Horrible Harry and the Ant Invasion

ALSO IN THIS SERIES

Horrible Harry in Room 2B
Horrible Harry and the Green Slime

HORRIBLE HARRY AND THE ANT INVASION

BY SUZY KLINE

Pictures by Frank Remkiewicz

SCHOLASTIC INC.

New York Toronto London Auckland Sydney

ISBN 0-590-43948-0

 Published by Scholastic Inc., 730 Broadway, New York, NY 10003, by arrangement with Viking Penguin, a division of Penguin Books USA Inc.

72 71 70 69 68 67 66 65 64 63 62 61 6 7 8 9/0

Printed in the U.S.A. 40

First Scholastic printing, March 1992

For my class who launched the original
ant invasion at Southwest School:

Vicki Aiken
Shannon Barriere
Justin Carile
Jennifer Condon
Gregory Dahlmann
Dawn DuCotey
Andrea Friday
Ricky Gaudette
Ryan Garofano
Elena Gelzinis
Michael George
Jimmy Grace
Dean Guenther
Shawn Hickey
Kim Milanese
Nathaniel Periera
Justin St. Pierre
Timothy Tribou

Contents

Horrible Harry and the Ant Invasion

When Harry and I walked into Room 2B, we couldn't believe our eyes.

"Look at that!" I said.

"Wow! What is it, Doug?" Harry asked me.

"It's an ant city."

"Ants . . ." Harry grinned. Then he rubbed his hands together.

Harry loves anything that crawls,

slithers, or slides. He loves slimy things, hairy things, and creepy things.

Harry loves anything horrible.

"The ants haven't arrived yet," Miss Mackle said. "But they should come any day now in the mail."

"The mail?" Sidney made a face. "Eewyee. There's going to be ants in Miss Mackle's mailbox."

Harry flashed his white teeth, "Neato . . ." he said. "Are we going to have an ant monitor?"

Miss Mackle looked at the list of jobs on the Monitor Chart. "We're going to need one. Would you be interested, Harry?"

Harry smiled so wide his silver filling showed in the back.

Miss Mackle printed Harry's name next to Ant Monitor.

One week later when the class was

lined up in the hall by the office, Miss Mackle checked her mailbox. She found a small manila envelope in it.

When she opened it up, she pulled out a plastic vial. There were a lot of black, hairy things moving around in it.

"THE ANTS!" the class shouted.

The school secretary, Mrs. Foxworth, poked her head around the corner. "Ants . . . ?" she replied.

“We’re going to observe their behavior,” Miss Mackle said.

Mrs. Foxworth tried to smile, but she was shaking so much the pencil that was sitting on her ear dropped to the floor.

Harry picked it up and handed it to her. “Are you afraid of ants?”

Mrs. Foxworth ran back to her typewriter.

Harry grinned. “She’s afraid of ants.”

“Well,” Miss Mackle said, “the direc-

tions on this small package say to put the vial in a refrigerator for ten minutes so the ants will go to sleep. It's easier to put sleeping ants in the ant city."

Harry stepped forward. "I'm the ant monitor. I'll take it to the teachers' refrigerator for you."

Miss Mackle raised her eyebrows.

"Can I pick an assistant?" Harry asked.

Miss Mackle nodded as she looked at the waving hands.

"I pick . . . Doug," Harry said.

I beamed.

Miss Mackle looked relieved.

We walked down the hall to the teachers' room with the vial of ants.

When we opened the refrigerator, we looked for a place to set the vial.

"Gee," I said, "there's so much diet soda in here, it's hard to find room."

Harry finally set the vial on top of a container of banana yogurt.

Then we walked back down the hall.

Mrs. Foxworth was coming toward us. "Hello, boys," she said in a cheery voice.

"Taking your morning break?" Harry asked.

Mrs. Foxworth nodded. "Thought I would have a little banana yogurt."

Harry and I stopped. We looked at each other.

Mrs. Foxworth closed the teachers' room door.

Then we heard it. A shrill scream!

Harry and I walked back to Room 2B laughing.

Ten minutes later Miss Mackle brought the vial of ants back to the classroom.

Everyone gathered around the science table. "I think I should do this, boys and girls," Miss Mackle said. "Some ants bite. I don't want *any* of you to touch one. Is that clear?"

Everyone nodded their heads.

Miss Mackle took the roof off an ant house. Then she took the cap off the vial. We all watched her pour the ants into the small opening.

"Their bodies look like raisins," Ida said.

"That's the way they sleep, Ida, all rolled up," Miss Mackle replied.

"Eewyee," Sidney groaned. "They're gross."

The teacher looked at Sidney. "We are scientists. We are observing ant behavior. Someday someone in Room 2B may be a great scientist and make great discoveries in a lab."

Harry and I pointed at each other. We

were planning to be great scientists. Someday.

Just as Miss Mackle finished pouring the sleeping ants into the hole, the ants at the bottom of the vial started to wake up.

"Goodness!" Miss Mackle exclaimed.

Sidney screamed when three ants crawled out of the vial onto the science table.

Miss Mackle stood up. "No one move or touch anything. I will get the ants."

"One is on the floor!" Mary called.

Miss Mackle crawled after it. She put a pencil in front of the runaway ant. It crawled up the eraser. Miss Mackle popped the ant into the opening of the ant house then put the roof back on.

"Two ants are missing," she said. Her hair was in her eyes and one of her high heels was off.

"THEY'RE GOING TO GET US!" Sidney shouted.

"Sidney," Miss Mackle said with her teeth clenched, "we *must* remain calm."

Harry stood in front of the teacher. "As your ant monitor, I will find the missing ants." And then he gave her a salute.

"Just *don't* touch the ants!" Miss Mackle insisted.

Harry took out his lunch box. He unwrapped his sandwich and scraped some peanut butter onto his finger.

Then he put his finger under the science table and waited.

Miss Mackle put her shoe back on, and pushed her hair out of her face. "I think everyone should return to their desks now."

"I found them!" Harry shouted from under the table.

Everyone bent down and looked.

Including Miss Mackle.

There were the two runaway ants on Harry's finger.

Miss Mackle grabbed her pencil and quickly scraped them off and then dropped them into the opening of the ant city.

Harry flashed a big smile. "I told you I'd find them."

Miss Mackle frowned. "I told you *not*

to touch the ants. Look at your finger."

Everyone did. There were two red marks.

"He got bit!" Mary exclaimed.

"I think you should go to the nurse," Miss Mackle said. "And when you come back you'll see another name on the Monitor Chart next to Ant Monitor."

Harry put his head down as he walked to the nurse's office.

The next morning, Harry was real quiet. He didn't join our conversation about ants at the science table.

"They bury their own dead," I said.

"They bury their own food," Mary said.

"Eewyee," Sidney replied. "Look, those ants are kissing!"

Miss Mackle walked over to our table. "Ants pass food by kissing. Sometimes they send messages that way."

Sidney fell off his chair and rolled over on the floor laughing.

"You may return to your seat, Sidney. Ida is about to feed the ants, and I want only serious scientists to watch."

Sidney frowned as he walked back to his chair.

Harry frowned as he watched Ida doing *his* job.

Ida filled an eye dropper from a bowl

of sugar water. Then when the teacher removed the roof, Ida squeezed the eye dropper three times into the ant house.

"I'll get it back," Harry whispered to me.

"Get what back?"

"My *ant monitor job*."

I looked at Harry. I could tell he was making plans.

"How?"

"All I have to do is get on the teacher's good side. Then I can ask her for another chance."

Just then Harry tipped back on his chair and his baseball cards came tumbling out of his pocket.

Miss Mackle put her hands on her hips. "Harry, put those things away. Baseball is a distraction in the classroom."

Harry got down on his knees and

picked up his baseball cards.

"I don't want any more antics from you today, Harry," Miss Mackle said.

"*Ant*ics?" Harry repeated. "That's an *ant* word."

Miss Mackle smiled. "Yes, it is. We have lots of ant words in our language. Maybe we should think of some."

Harry clapped his hands.

Mmmmmm, I thought. Harry might just pull it off.

"I'll start," Miss Mackle said. "*Ant*i-freeze; I had to put some in my car this morning."

"*Ant*arctica and Atl*ant*ic," Mary said, looking at the globe.

"Good, any others?" the teacher asked.

"*Ant*ipasto," Mr. Cardini, the principal, said as he showed up at the door.

Everyone laughed.

"My mother makes the best antipasto in the world—salami, cheese, black olives, mmmmmm. Just stopped in to visit the ants," he said sitting down at the science table.

Miss Mackle continued the lesson.

"Eleph*ant* and p*ant*her," I said, thinking about animals in the zoo.

Harry held up *Jack and the Beanstalk*. "Gi*ant*!"

Miss Mackle wrote the new words on the board.

"Fancy," Ida said.

"Nice try, but that doesn't have a *t* in it," Miss Mackle said.

"Ranch?" Sidney asked.

"That is a *c-h* word."

Our class seemed to be stuck.

Then Mr. Cardini saw two ants kissing and he stood up. "I've got one—ro*mant*ic!"

Everyone groaned as he waltzed out of the room.

"*I've* got the best ant word," Harry said. Then he pointed to the December calendar. "S*ant*a!"

Everyone cheered and clapped.

Then Harry stood up like he had the biggest idea in the world. "Why don't we draw pictures of ants carrying these words? We could make them go up the stairway and invade the second floor!"

Invasions, I thought. Harry loved them.

Miss Mackle looked at the long list of ant words on the board.

"Let's do it!" she said.

Everyone took out their crayons and scissors as the teacher passed out brown paper.

"I'm making a black ant to carry my word, p*ant*her," I said.

"I'm making a HUGE ant to carry my word, gi*ant*," Harry said.

"I'm making a big red heart next to my ant," Mary replied.

Everyone knew what ant word Mary was doing. Rom*ant*ic.

When all the ants were drawn and cut, and the words were neatly printed above, the class lined up in the hall.

Miss Mackle walked us to the stairwell. "Let's hope we have enough to make it to the top!"

"We will!" Harry called out. Then he whispered to me. "We have to. She'll be in such a good mood, she'll give me another chance to be ant monitor."

We started taping the ants at the bottom of the wall near the stairs and made a trail going up and down and around the stairway.

GIANT
Romantic
PANTHER

When we got to the top, we were one word short.

Everyone sat down on the stairs.

"I knew we couldn't do it," Sidney complained.

"Well," Miss Mackle replied, "maybe tomorrow."

Harry made a face. Then he reached in his back pocket and pulled out three baseball cards. "The Yankees! They won the penn*ant* this year."

"AN ANT WORD!" everyone shouted.

Miss Mackle clapped her hands. "Bravo, Harry! You can make the word today and put it up. WE reached the second floor thanks to . . ." and she looked at Harry's baseball cards, "some distractions!"

Harry beamed at his teacher. "If I promise to follow your directions in science, will you give me another chance to be ant monitor?"

Miss Mackle put her hand on Harry's shoulder and smiled. "All right, Harry. I don't see why you *can't*."

Harry was horribly happy.

Horrible Harry and the Square Dance

Miss Mackle stood in front of the room. "This Friday we are going to have a square dance."

All the boys groaned.

Except Harry.

I knew what Harry was thinking. He wanted to dance with Song Lee.

Harry has had a crush on Song Lee since kindergarten. That's when she brought in a potato beetle for show-and-tell.

She didn't say anything but she passed a box around with a small striped bug in it.

Harry looked at the bug, then at Song Lee.

It was true love.

Friday afternoon, Miss Mackle led our class down to the gym. She had a record under her arm. It was the "Virginia Reel."

"Now," she said. "I want the boys to line up behind Sidney, and the girls to line up behind Mary."

"I don't want to dance with her," Sidney said, looking at Mary across from him.

Miss Mackle put the record down and then she looked at Sidney. She had her hands on her hips.

"Sidney, one of the reasons I have dancing is that we need to learn manners."

Sidney put his head down.

"We must say thank you to everyone we dance with. Being polite is very important."

After a moment of silence, Miss Mackle added. "ANYBODY who doesn't agree can dance with the teacher after school—when we'll go over these rules."

Sidney turned green.

All the girls giggled.

All the boys groaned. I did, too. Dancing with the teacher would be deadly.

Miss Mackle showed the girls how to curtsy.

Then she showed the boys how to bow.

Everyone practiced.

I made a face. I hate to dance. When I looked across the floor, I looked at my partner.

It was Song Lee.

Harry gave me a jab in the side. "Move over," he said. "I'm dancing with her."

I didn't mind at all. There were more boys than girls, and no one was standing next to Song Lee.

"You have Miss X," Miss Mackle said to me.

I beamed. Dancing with no one wasn't bad at all.

Miss Mackle then showed us how to do the Virginia reel.

Harry walked over and took Song Lee's hands. He wanted to get ready early.

"Not yet," Miss Mackle said. "I haven't even turned the music on."

Everyone laughed.

Harry held up his fist.

When the music finally did go on, the boys walked across the floor and bowed.

The girls walked across the floor and curtsied.

"Now let's do the Virginia reel!" Miss Mackle called.

Sidney walked over and took Mary's hands. His eyes were closed.

They sashayed down the center.

And then they joined their lines.

"You didn't stop and twirl her under your arm," Miss Mackle complained.

Harry was next.

He walked over and took Song Lee's hands and then they sashayed down the center. He stopped, put up his arm, and Song Lee twirled around and then curtsied.

Harry bowed so low his curly hair touched his knees.

"Bravo!" Miss Mackle said.

Harry flashed his white teeth.

Song Lee looked down at her black shoes.

When I came down with Miss X, everyone laughed.

The next time we went through the line we had new partners. I had Ida. Sidney had Song Lee.

When Sidney went over to take Song Lee's hands, he had his eyes closed again. He didn't want to dance with a girl.

Instead of looking where he was going, he walked right into her, and they bumped heads.

Song Lee put her hand on her forehead. There was a big bump and red mark on her forehead. She was trying not to cry but everyone could see the tears on her cheek.

Harry raised a fist at Sidney.

Miss Mackle sent Song Lee to the nurse. Then she said, "We will have one more dance. Sidney, you must be more careful."

"He should keep his eyes open," I said.

Miss Mackle walked over to Sidney. "Were you dancing with your eyes closed?"

Sidney shook his head. "Nope. They were wide open all the time like this."

The class stared at Sidney's eyes. They looked like giant white gumballs. Then he made them revolve around and around.

Miss Mackle turned to put the needle on the record.

Harry raised two fists. I knew what he was thinking. Double revenge.

When we returned to the classroom, Song Lee was sitting in her chair with

an ice bottle held against her forehead.

Just before the three o'clock bell rang, Harry offered to take the bottle back to the nurse for her.

Song Lee thanked him and then went out of the classroom to get her coat.

As the rest of the class lined up to go home, Harry said, "Hey, Sidney. Meet me at the corner. I have a little present for you."

"You do?" Sidney said.

Harry flashed his white teeth. "I do."

Sidney waited for Harry at the corner. "What are you giving me a present for?" he asked when he saw Harry.

"For that trick you did in dancing today."

"Trick?" Sidney couldn't remember.

"You bumped into Song Lee because your eyes were shut."

"Yeah! She even had to go to the nurse with the alligator purse!" Sidney said, bursting into laughter. "So where's my present?"

"Right here," Harry said, flipping the ice bottle and pouring it down Sidney's back.

"Yeoooooow! *That's* COLD!" Sidney screamed as he ran up the street waving his hands in the air. "I'll get even with you for this. Just wait!"

I looked at Harry. "Where did you get that bottle of ice water?"

"From Song Lee. I told her I would return the bottle to the nurse."

And then Harry flashed his white teeth. "I didn't say I would return the melted ice inside."

I cracked up.

"Ol' Sidney had it coming," Harry mumbled.

I waited at the school's steps while Harry returned the empty bottle to the nurse.

Sometimes when Harry tells you he's going to do something, he leaves the horrible part out.

Horrible Harry and the Deadly Fish Tank

We have a fish tank in Room 2B. Last time Harry and I counted there were twenty-five fish swimming around in it.

Twenty guppies.

Four neon fish.

And one black molly.

Then there was horrible Monday. This is how it happened.

Sidney came to school mad. He was

mad about Harry putting ice water down his back on Friday.

Even his hair looked angry. It stood on end. Sidney probably didn't bother combing it.

Miss Mackle looked at the Monitor Chart. "Boys and girls, I will announce the week's new monitors. Sidney is Messenger, Doug is Paper Monitor, Ida is Ant Monitor, Mary is Plant Monitor, Song Lee is Sweeper, and . . ." when she finally got to Harry she said, "Harry is Fish Monitor."

Harry immediately got up and went back to feed the fish. He turned on the light in the tank and took roll. Carefully he recorded the number in the Fish Roll Book.

Then he checked the temperature. It was in the green part of the thermometer—in the 70–80 degree range.

At lunchtime, Harry fed the fish and then lined up behind me in the cafeteria. "I have my favorite dessert, Doug," he said. "Two pieces of Mom's homemade fudge. I'm saving it for us on the way home from school."

I drooled. I knew how good Harry's mother's fudge was. Chocolate, nutty, and mmmmmmmm good.

After lunch when we were working on math, Harry walked back to check the tank. The he shouted, "The black molly is floating on the water. She's DEAD!"

Everyone rushed back to the tank.

Miss Mackle opened the cover of the tank and took out the net. She scooped up the dead fish. Then she put her finger in the water. "Why, the water is hot! Someone has been fooling with the temperature knob."

Everyone looked at the thermometer. The mercury was way above the green zone. "Who would do such a horrible thing?" Miss Mackle exclaimed.

Everyone looked at Harry.

I did too. Harry loves to do horrible things.

Miss Mackle waited for someone to speak.

Sidney spoke first. "Harry is the fish monitor. He did it!"

"Do you know anything about this?" Miss Mackle asked Harry.

Harry shook his head.

Miss Mackle said we wouldn't be doing "little theater" that afternoon. She didn't feel like doing anything fun. She was too disappointed.

We just worked at our seats the rest of the afternoon.

It was a long day.

When Harry lined up at three o'clock, no one wanted to stand next to him.

Except me.

"Do you think I did it?" Harry asked as we walked home.

I didn't say anything. I wasn't sure.

"Doug," Harry said. "I wouldn't do anything *that* horrible. I plan on being a great scientist someday. With you, remember? I would never take the life of a single living thing. Not a beetle, or an ant, or a single blade of grass."

I knew Harry never mowed the lawn. He told his mother he couldn't kill the grass.

We walked home without talking. We didn't even eat Harry's homemade fudge. We just didn't feel like it. The next morning, Harry made a poster and put it up by the fish tank. It was a picture of a tombstone and a graveyard. It said GOD BLESS R BLAK MOLLY.

Then in the top part was a bunch of fish with yellow wings and halos flying around.

"What's that up there?" I asked.

"Fish heaven," Harry replied.

Miss Mackle started the morning as usual with a conversation.

"Boys and girls, we need to talk about our fish. We are responsible for them. Somehow, we made an error."

Sidney raised his hand. "Harry is the

fish monitor. He likes to do horrible things. Harry did it. He should stay after school." Then he sat back in his chair and smiled.

I looked at Sidney. Then it dawned on me. Revenge. That's what Sidney wanted! He wanted to get even because Harry had put ice water down his back.

Harry raised his fist at Sidney. "I wouldn't cook a fish like that."

"Prove it!" Sidney replied.

"Harry," Miss Mackle said, "do you know anything about how the black molly died?"

Harry shook his head.

Everyone made a face. No one believed Harry but me.

"Did anyone see someone at the fish tank just before the lunch bell? I asked.

Song Lee had her hand in the air for the *first* time.

"Yes, Song Lee," Miss Mackle said. "Did you see someone?"

Softly, Song Lee spoke, "I see Sidney by the tank just before bell ring. He reach behind where knob is."

Sidney sank down in his chair.

Miss Mackle glared at him.

Sidney looked at the teacher, then the class. His face turned red. "I didn't

mean to kill the fish. I just . . . just . . ."

"Just what?" Miss Mackle asked.

". . . wanted to get . . ." Sidney's voice got softer and softer ". . . Harry in trouble."

"We'll talk about it after school," Miss Mackle said firmly.

Harry looked over at Song Lee.

And beamed.

Harry really isn't *that* horrible. On a scale of 1–10, he probably is a 7 for horribleness.

Then I noticed Harry got up and got his lunch box. He took something out of it and gave it to Song Lee.

It was the two pieces of homemade fudge!

Forget that 7. Anyone who gives *my* fudge away to a *girl* is a 10!

Horrible Harry and the Class Picture

Tuesday everyone came to school looking very neat. It was picture day for Room 2B.

"How nice everyone looks!" Miss Mackle exclaimed.

We looked at the teacher's hairdo. It was real curly. And it looked red.

"Did you dye your hair?" Mary asked the teacher.

Miss Mackle's face turned red. "No, I just . . ." Her voice got softer ". . . just used a red rinse."

"You look pretty," Harry said. And then he flashed his white teeth.

"Thank you, Harry, you look quite nice in your suit and tie."

"My mother made me wear it. She's ordering pictures for all my relatives for Christmas."

"Will we get free combs this year?" Sidney blurted out.

"Let's hope so," Mary said. "You need one."

Everyone looked at Sidney. His hair stuck out all over his head.

Miss Mackle took out her red attendance book. "Let's see, everyone is here today except . . . Song Lee?"

We looked around. She wasn't at her desk or next to the fish tank or sharpening a pencil.

Harry frowned. "Do you think she's sick?"

"I hope not," Miss Mackle said. "It would be so nice to have everyone present for the picture."

Just then, Song Lee appeared at the door.

Harry's eyebrows shot up.

Miss Mackle went to meet her. "Why, Song Lee, you look beautiful."

Song Lee looked down at the floor. Her hair was in a bun. Two white flowers were pinned on either side of her hair.

She was wearing a long dress and a flowered sash. When Song Lee looked up she said, "Mother want to send picture to Korea for my relatives."

Miss Mackle smiled. "They will be very pleased."

Just then Mrs. Foxworth appeared at the door. "The photographer is ready for Room 2B in the gym now."

As we walked down the hall, I said to Harry, "We probably won't get to stand next to each other. I'm four inches taller than you."

"I know," Harry replied. "I'll probably be next to the king of hairdos."

I knew who Harry meant.

Sidney.

"Maybe you'll get lucky," I said.

"What do you mean?" Harry asked.

"You might be next to Song Lee."

Harry looked at me and grinned.

"You might be next to the teacher," Harry said.

I frowned.

When we got in the gym, a mother

passed out orange combs. Another mother went up to each student and helped to comb their hair. When she got to Sidney, she couldn't get his snarls out.

Then the comb broke.

"Okay, kiddies!" the photographer said. "Line up over here."

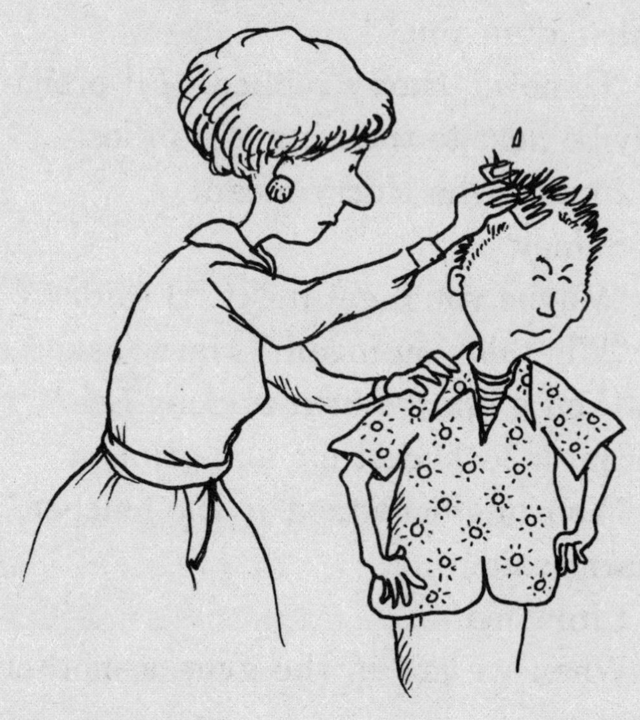

When he saw Harry in his suit and Song Lee in her outfit, he said, "Oh la la! Look who's getting married today!"

Everyone laughed and giggled.

Harry held up a fist. "I'm going to be a great scientist when I grow up. I'm not getting married."

Song Lee kept looking at her sash.

"Well, you two make a great couple. You can hold the sign that says, MISS MACKLE'S SECOND GRADE CLASS."

Sidney cackled so loud, he was hurting my eardrums.

"And you two gorgeous redheads can stand together!" the photographer said.

Then he moved Sidney and the teacher together.

Everyone laughed again. Except Sidney.

"Hey, good looking," the photographer said to me, "you get to stand between two lovely ladies."

I made a face and stood between Ida and Mary.

"Okay, kiddies," the photographer said. "Say hamburger with pickles and cheese!"

The photographer flashed his camera.

"Now say liver and onions!"

The photographer flashed his camera again.

I was hoping the picture would be over real soon. I was surrounded by girls.

"Say spaghetti and meatballs!"

The photographer flashed his camera one last time.

"I hope I didn't close my eyes," Miss Mackle said.

Harry put the sign down on the floor. Then he lined up by the ramp.

I could tell Harry was miffed about something. He took off his tie and stuffed it in his pocket.

When I stood next to him, he whispered. "I don't like that guy."

"You mean the photographer?"

Harry nodded.

"Yeah," I said. "I think he should open a restaurant and sell liver and onions, spaghetti and meatballs, and hamburgers with pickles."

Harry looked at me and then at the photographer. "That guy was acting so dumb I wouldn't buy a picture *or* a pickle from him."

Harry always tells the horrible truth.

ABOUT THE AUTHOR

Suzy Kline graduated from the University of California at Berkeley and received her elementary school teacher's credential from California State University at Hayward. She has been teaching for sixteen years and is the author of the popular Herbie Jones series (available in Puffin). Kline was selected Teacher of the Year in 1986 by the Torrington School District in Connecticut and in 1988 by the Probus Club of Torrington.

Kline is married and has two daughters. Her husband's first book, *Watch Out for These Weirdos*, will be coming out soon from Viking.